Mousekin's
Birth

MOUSEKIN'S BIRTH

(Originally titled MOUSEKIN'S
WOODLAND BIRTHDAY)

Story and pictures by
EDNA MILLER

PRENTICE-HALL, Inc., Englewood Cliffs, N.J.

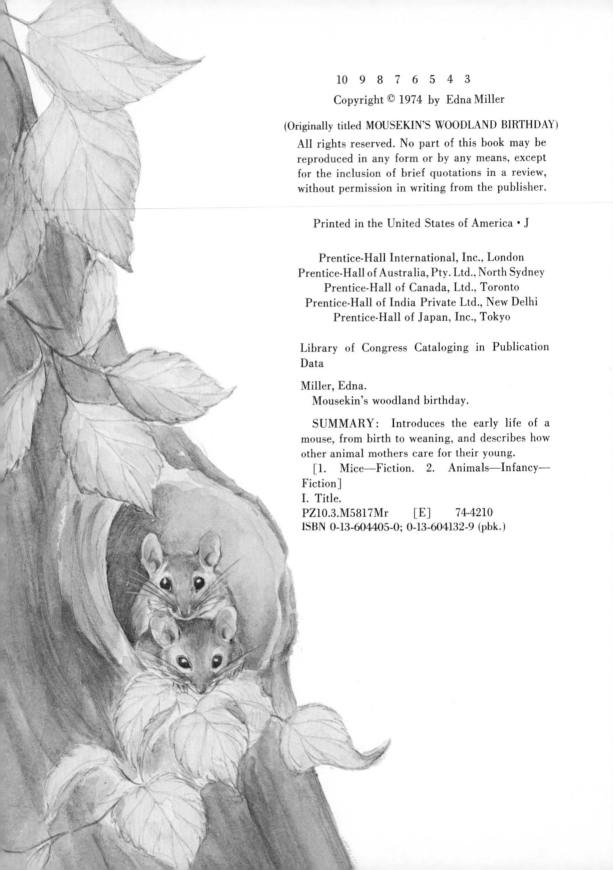

10 9 8 7 6 5 4 3

Copyright © 1974 by Edna Miller

(Originally titled MOUSEKIN'S WOODLAND BIRTHDAY)

Printed in the United States of America • J

Prentice-Hall International, Inc., London
Prentice-Hall of Australia, Pty. Ltd., North Sydney
Prentice-Hall of Canada, Ltd., Toronto
Prentice-Hall of India Private Ltd., New Delhi
Prentice-Hall of Japan, Inc., Tokyo

Library of Congress Cataloging in Publication Data

Miller, Edna.
  Mousekin's woodland birthday.

  SUMMARY: Introduces the early life of a mouse, from birth to weaning, and describes how other animal mothers care for their young.
  [1. Mice—Fiction. 2. Animals—Infancy—Fiction]
I. Title.
PZ10.3.M5817Mr   [E]   74-4210
ISBN 0-13-604405-0; 0-13-604132-9 (pbk.)

In the time it takes a sparrow
to blink its eye,
Mousekin began to grow.
In that instant
when father's sperm
met mother's egg
within his mother's body,
all the things that make a mouse
a mouse
had happened.

He would be a soft furry creature
with large silken ears,
bright shoe-button eyes,
and dainty white paws;
a timid night creature,
as all other white-footed mice
had been before him.

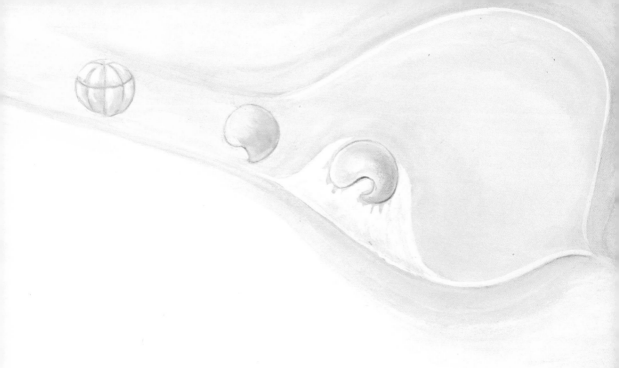

He was, at first, a tiny fertile egg,
smaller than a mustard seed.
He divided once, twice, again and again,
until he became a hollow ball
of millions of mouse cells.
The ball of cells
(which would be Mousekin)
traveled along a passageway
into his mother's womb.

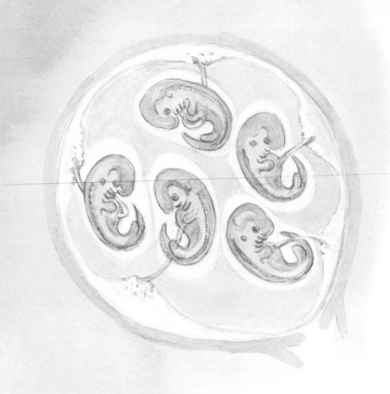

Attached in the soft warm chamber,
his mother's body
would nourish him
while he grew to baby size.
Mousekin was not alone in his mother's womb.
Two brothers and two sisters
shared his quiet world
and grew as fast as he.

Mother and father searched the forest
for some abandoned home.
They had to find some quiet place,
as safe and as warm as a mother's body,
to cradle their babies when they were born.

Other furry creatures had babies of their own.
A fox mother was much too busy with her kits
to spy a pair of white-footed mice
as they peeked into her den.

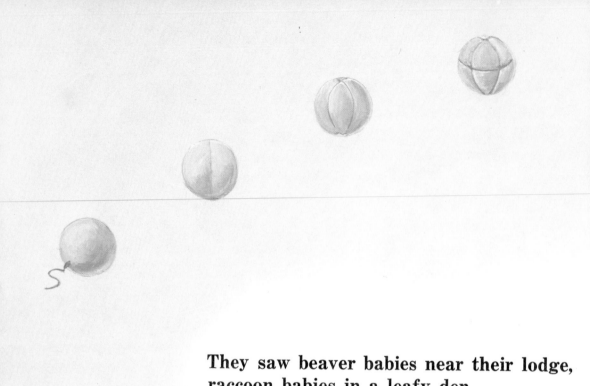

They saw beaver babies near their lodge,
raccoon babies in a leafy den.

Each had begun its life, as Mousekin had,
a single fertile egg
within its mother's body.

The mice found a woodchuck's empty home.
It was much too large.

A wren's nest was high and safe
but it was much too small.
A chipmunk's house was just the right size
for a white-footed family.

In the twenty-one days it takes a mouse to grow
from egg to baby size,
mother and father had lined their nest
with softest cattail down.
One day, while carrying bits of moss,
mother mouse felt her babies stir.
They had grown enough to live outside
and wanted to be free.

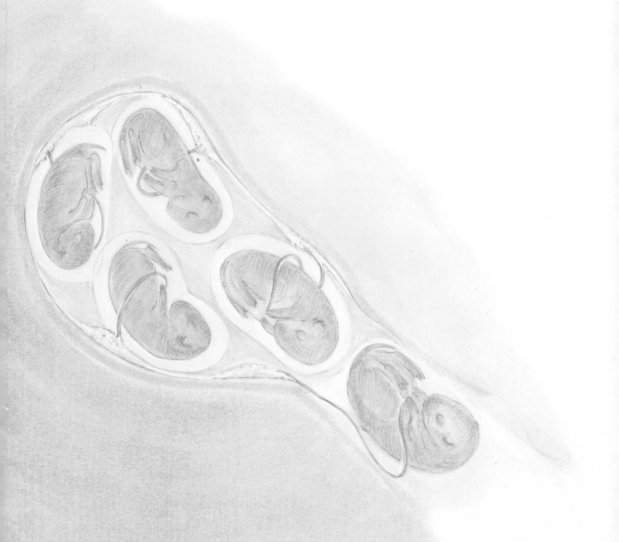

One by one the babies moved
down the passageway
from the dark and peaceful world
they'd known
to the quiet of the nest.
Mother mouse cleaned each tiny form
as it arrived.
Mousekin came first—
a squirming, pink, mouse baby,
no larger than a bumble bee.
He found a teat on his mother's underbelly.
In the furry warmth
he drank his first drop of mouse milk.

Days passed quickly in the nest.
The little mice grew strong.
Each had a coat of soft gray fur
and a pair of jet-black eyes.
One day, as mother cuddled them,
she heard strange sounds above.
Heavy footsteps shook the ground
and bits of gravel fell.

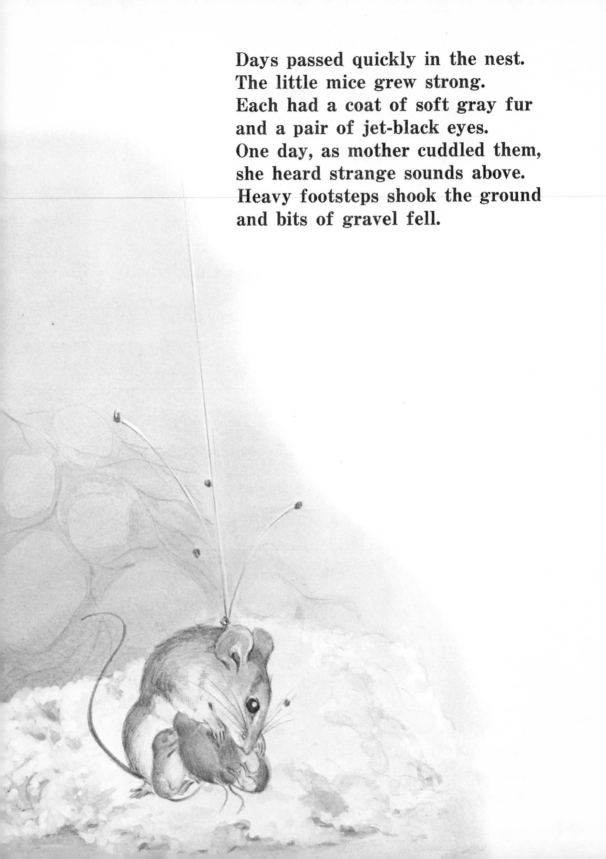

Alone with her young,
mother mouse was frightened.
(Mouse fathers leave the nest
'til baby mice have grown.)
When all her babies were asleep,
still gripping her teats,
she stretched to peer outside.
When all seemed safe
and nothing moved
she raced from the nest
as fast as she could
with five mouse babies hanging on.

She ran past the fiddleheads
and marsh marigolds.
Traveling over a fallen log,
two babies lost their hold.
Mother mouse snatched one baby
and carried it in her mouth.
She could not carry anymore
in her frantic flight.
Mousekin was left behind.

Mousekin sat very still.
His mother would come for him.
Above, and all around him,
was a great new world to see.
There were birds and insects overhead.
From his hiding place
beside the fallen log,
he could see fish in clear blue water.

While Mousekin waited for his mother
he watched a turtle make her nest.
Thrashing the ground with strong hind legs
and swinging her shelled body
from side to side,
the box turtle laid many round, white eggs.

When the turtle had covered her eggs
and was about to move away,
she turned to Mousekin and slowly said,
"Not all creatures are born alive.
Some are *hatched* from eggs."

Without moving from his hiding place,
beside the fallen log,
Mousekin could see eggs of every size and shape.
He saw insect eggs on a leafy twig,
clusters of fish eggs in shallow water,

and bird eggs, brightly colored,
in a low hanging nest.

Only bird babies, newly hatched,
cried loudly for their mother.

Mousekin was hungry too.
He nibbled a bud on a nearby branch
and tasted some tender shoots of grass.

While he tried the strange new foods
SOMETHING bounced beside him;
much bigger than a turtle's egg
and every rainbow color!

He pressed his body to the ground
and never moved a whisker.
As footsteps thundered near
Mousekin squeaked.
In an instant mother mouse was at his side.
He felt her gentle grip.

In leaps and bounds she carried him
into a hollow tree.

Brothers and sisters welcomed him
with happy squeaks and squeals.
Before the babies settled down,
Mousekin peered outside.
Perhaps the frightening sights and sounds
were woodland babies too.